Copyright © 2013 by NordSüd Verlag AG, CH-8005 Zürich, Switzerland.
First published in Switzerland under the title *Ritter Wüterich und Drache Borste*.
English text copyright © 2013 by NorthSouth Books Inc., New York 10016.
Translated by David Henry Wilson.

First published in the United States, Great Britain, Canada, Australia, and New Zealand in 2013 by NorthSouth Books, Inc., an imprint of NordSüd Verlag AG, CH-8005 Zürich, Switzerland.

Distributed in the United States by NorthSouth Books Inc., New York 10016.
Library of Congress Cataloging-in-Publication Data is available.
ISBN: 978-0-7358-4110-9 (trade edition).
Printed in Germany by Grafisches Centrum Cuno GmbH & Co. KG, 39240 Calbe, November 2012.

1 3 5 7 9 • 10 8 6 4 2
www.northsouth.com

The ANGRY Little Knight

Annette Langen
Illustrated by Katja Gehrmann

**North
South**

In the middle of
Knightland stood
a giant castle.

It had a real moat, real watchtowers, and real guards who stood looking, day and night, for dangerous dragons.

In the castle lived a little knight who had a very bad temper. He had lots of noble names, just like his ancestors. He was called Sir Henry Oliver Theodor Herbert Egbert Albert Dewinterbottom. But his parents called him **HOTHEAD** for short . . . and that's exactly what he was.

Hothead had nearly everything a real knight needs:
    a shining suit of armor with a helmet,
    a shield to ward off nasty blows,
    a silver sword, a sharp dagger, a long lance,
    and, last but not least, his swift smart steed, Roswitha.
    But his weapons were much too **HEAVY** for such
a small knight. And so he had a servant who followed
him around carrying all his things for him.

There was only one place where the hot-tempered knight went without his weapons and his servant. And that place was the little boys' room.

Otherwise, he always wore his helmet with its fiery red feather. That had been given to him by the king himself—for his knightly courage in battle.

There was just one problem. Sir Hothead's battles were never anything but practice. He had never had a single real adventure of his own. He simply didn't have the time.

1. Sword
2. Dagger
3. Lance
4. Sword
5. LUNCH
6. Dagger
7. Lance
8. Sword

Sir Hothead was too busy practicing. And what he practiced was fighting, because there were enemies everywhere. First he would be on guard with the sword, then attack with the dagger, and finally, with a great roar, charge with the lance. So it went on, day after day, and no doubt it would have continued like that forever.

Until one day, from the deep dark forest there arose great clouds of smoke. The dragons were having fun. Sir Hothead stopped in his tracks. He had had enough of fighting scarecrows, dolls, and dummies.

Sir Hothead roared like a lion with a tummyache: "As sure as I'm hot, I'll show 'em what's what!" And in his rage, he hurled his shield, his sword, his dagger, and his lance against the castle wall, which rattled like a sheet of tin.

The worst criminals in the deepest dungeons trembled with terror. The castle ghost fled with a shiver to the kitchen. There the royal cook dropped the saltshaker straight in the soup.

And in the throne room, the king and queen stopped whatever they were doing and cried, "What on Earth is our little Hothead up to now?"

What did they see and hear?

"I'm finished and done with all this practice!" raged Hothead. "I want a real adventure!" He jumped onto his trusty steed, Roswitha, and galloped out through the castle gate—without a single weapon!

The king rushed up to the top of the watchtower. He looked across the deep dark forest and saw the cloud of smoke. He shook his head and gasped, "Dragons are not to be trifled with."

Mama Dragon was looking at the castle, from where all that terrible noise had just come. "Little Hothead must be throwing another tantrum," she hissed, nervously twitching her tail. She was nervous because she didn't know where her dragon son, Dripdry, had gone.

Dripdry was wandering all alone through the forest. But the farther he went, the darker it became. The branches of the trees looked like sharp claws that were trying to seize him. The wind whistled eerily, and his skin became all goose bumpy and his teeth chattered like ice cubes. Then the young dragon heard something else: horse's hooves that were racing nearer and nearer.

Who could it be?

It was none other than Sir Hothead himself. Red with rage, he rode his steed, Roswitha, through the dark forest. Suddenly, the horse dug all four hooves into the ground, and Hothead flew over her head like a cannonball and landed—*plunk!*—on a rock of fiery red.

"**Hic!**" said something underneath him.

"Ugh, what's that?" cried Hothead. Never before had he sat on a rock that had hiccups. He quickly lifted the visor of his helmet and looked around. "Hm, it's got bristly ears like a dragon, dirty teeth like a dragon, and . . ."—he slid down the red rock and held his nose— ". . . stinky feet like a dragon!" Then his face went very white.

He was standing in front of a **GIGANTIC LITTLE DRAGON**.
"Gallons of grimy goo!" growled Dripdry. "Just look at you, you little tin can! You stink of soap." He stuck out his giant snout and had a good sniff at Hothead. "And . . . hmmmm . . . cake!" **Hic!**

"What a rotten time to have hiccups. In order to get rid of them, dragons do three things: they roar and thump their chests . . . **hic** . . . blow down five trees . . . **hic** . . . and gobble seven rocks."

But . . . **hic** . . . none of these tricks worked for Dripdry.

HIC

Suddenly, Hothead's fiery red feather, awarded to him for his knightly courage, trembled on his helmet. The wind howled through the dark forest. Or was it ghosts? Or, even worse, robbers? The knight and the dragon both froze. The only movement was Dripdry's chattering teeth. The fiery red feather went fluttering through the air, but Hothead caught it.

Hothead held the feather in his hand and tickled the young dragon.
Dripdry forgot all about his hiccups and squealed, "Stop it! I'm very
tickl . . ." But he didn't finish his sentence, because . . . **ACHOO!**
He sneezed out a thick black cloud of smoke.

All at once the little knight looked as black as a piece of charcoal. He howled with rage. "Now look what you've done to my shiny armor!" he roared. He was so angry that he was ready to go home immediately.

Dripdry begged him to stay. "Please play with me!" he pleaded. Hothead sulked in silence.

"Oh well, I'm going swimming," announced Dripdry, and raced away with giant strides.

"Hey, wait for me!" cried Hothead. The last thing he wanted was to stay alone in the gloom.

But he didn't have to. Dripdry carried him on his back. The dark forest didn't seem nearly so dark when there were two of them. The branches no longer looked like sharp claws that made their teeth chatter and gave them goose bumps and hiccups.

"First one into the water is the winner!" roared Dripdry.

And the little knight and the young dragon splished and splashed in the water, until suddenly both of them felt very hungry. Fortunately, the clever Roswitha had brought along some sausages-on-the-sword and sausages-on-the-spear to put an end to all the tummy rumblings.

"Make sure you don't burn them!" Hothead warned Dripdry.

The young dragon grilled them with a single burst of flame. Then he had a good sniff and took a big bite. Mmm, the grilled sausages tasted even better than granite balls with lava sauce.

When they had finished eating the last delicious morsel, Hothead climbed onto his trusty steed, Roswitha. "Hey, Dripdry, shall we play again tomorrow? We'll bring some more sausages!"

The young dragon's nose tickled with anticipation, which made him sneeze out a thick black cloud of soot. That, though, was as good as saying "Okay!"

That evening, when Sir Hothead rode
back over the drawbridge to the castle,
he was so covered in soot that his parents
hardly recognized him. But now he knew
exactly what real knights have to have:
  adventures (and there were lots more
    to come),
  a swift smart steed like Roswitha,
  a few trials by fire,
  and a friend who could make the
    dark forest seem a lot brighter.